W9-BAB-737

For my dearest Rikka

 Published by Scholastic Inc., 555 Broadway,
New York, NY 10012, by arrangement with Candlewick Press.
The pictures for this book were done in watercolor, crayon, and pencil.
Printed in the U.S.A.
ISBN 0-590-67899-X

3 4 5 6 7 8 9 10 08 02 01 00 99

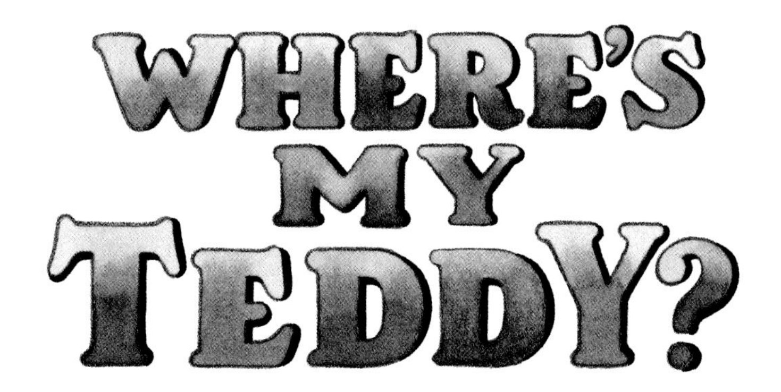

by Jez Alborough

SCHOLASTIC INC.
New York Toronto London Auckland Sydney

Eddie's off to find his teddy.
Eddie's teddy's name is Freddie.

He lost him in the woods somewhere.
It’s dark and horrible in there.

“Help!” said Eddie. “I’m scared already!
I want my bed! I want my teddy!”

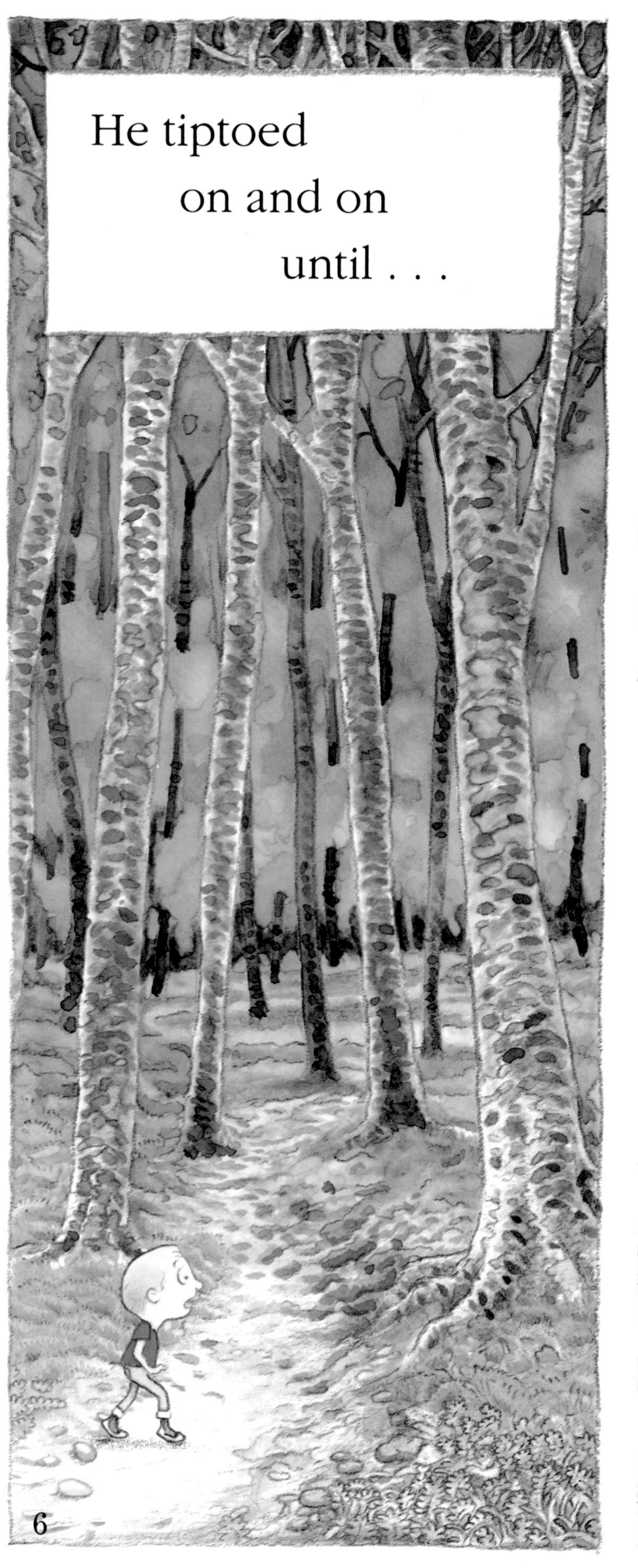
He tiptoed
on and on
until . . .

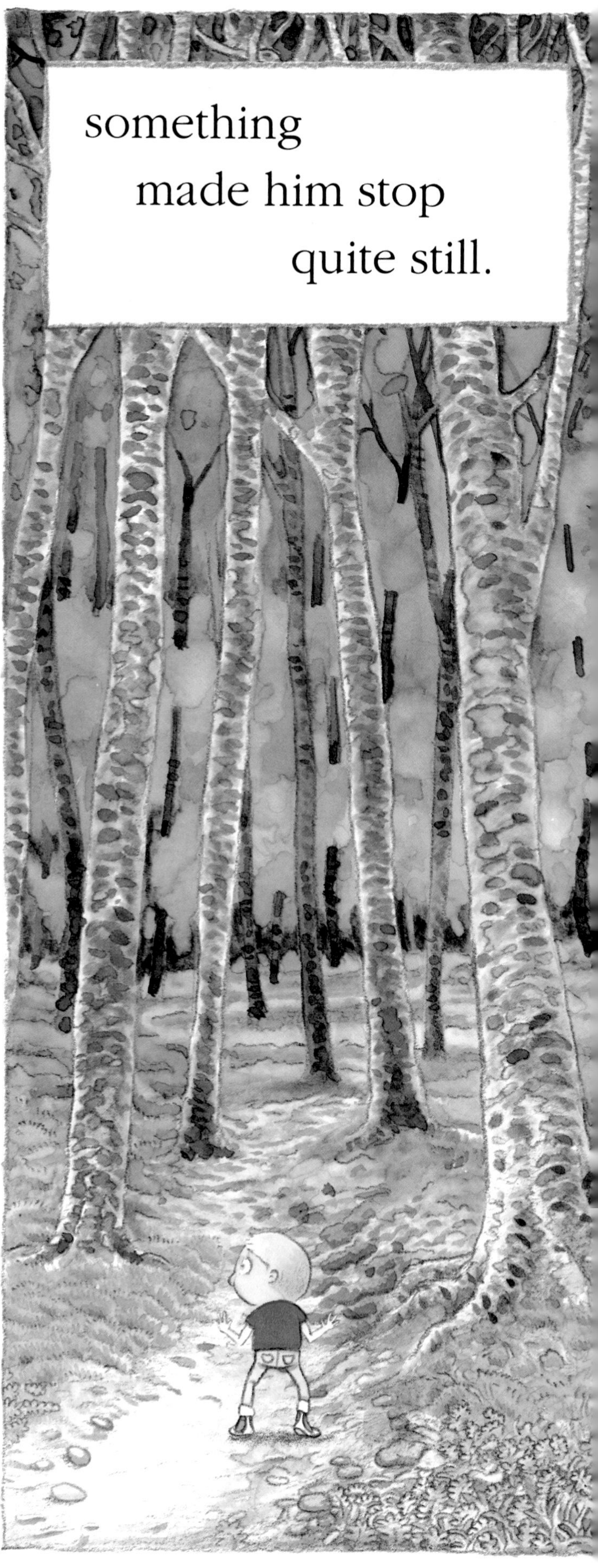
something
made him stop
quite still.

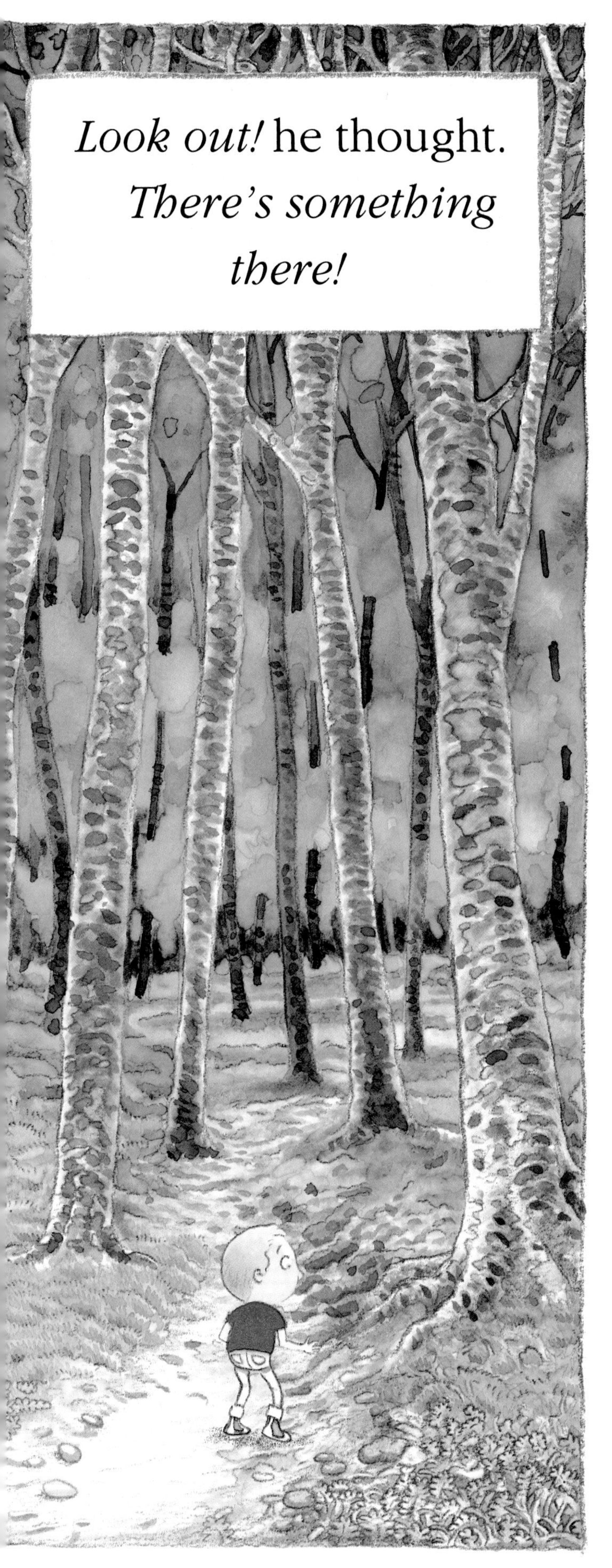
Look out! he thought.
There's something there!

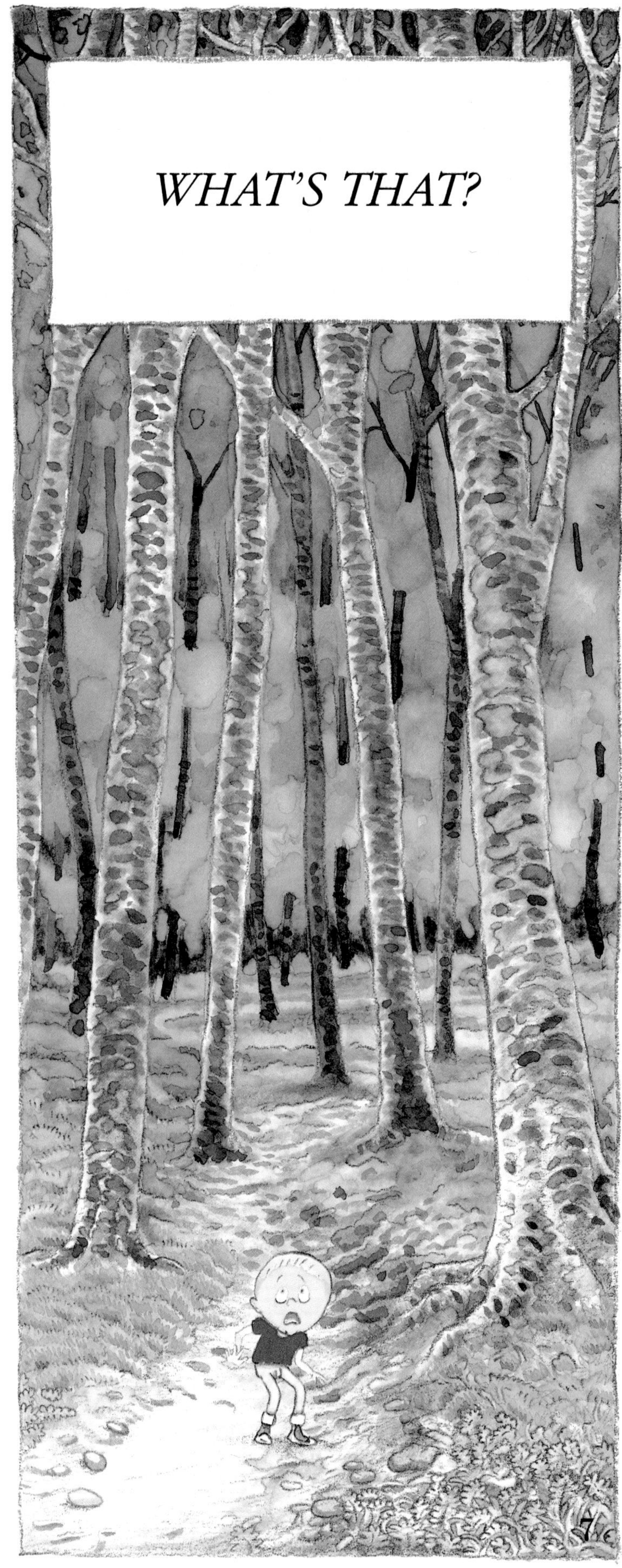
WHAT'S THAT?

A GIANT TEDDY BEAR!
“Is it Freddie?” said Eddie.
“What a surprise!
How *did* you get to be this size?”

“You’re too big to huddle and cuddle,” he said,

“and I’ll never fit both of us into my bed.”

Then out of the darkness,
clearer and clearer,
the sound of sobbing
came nearer and nearer.

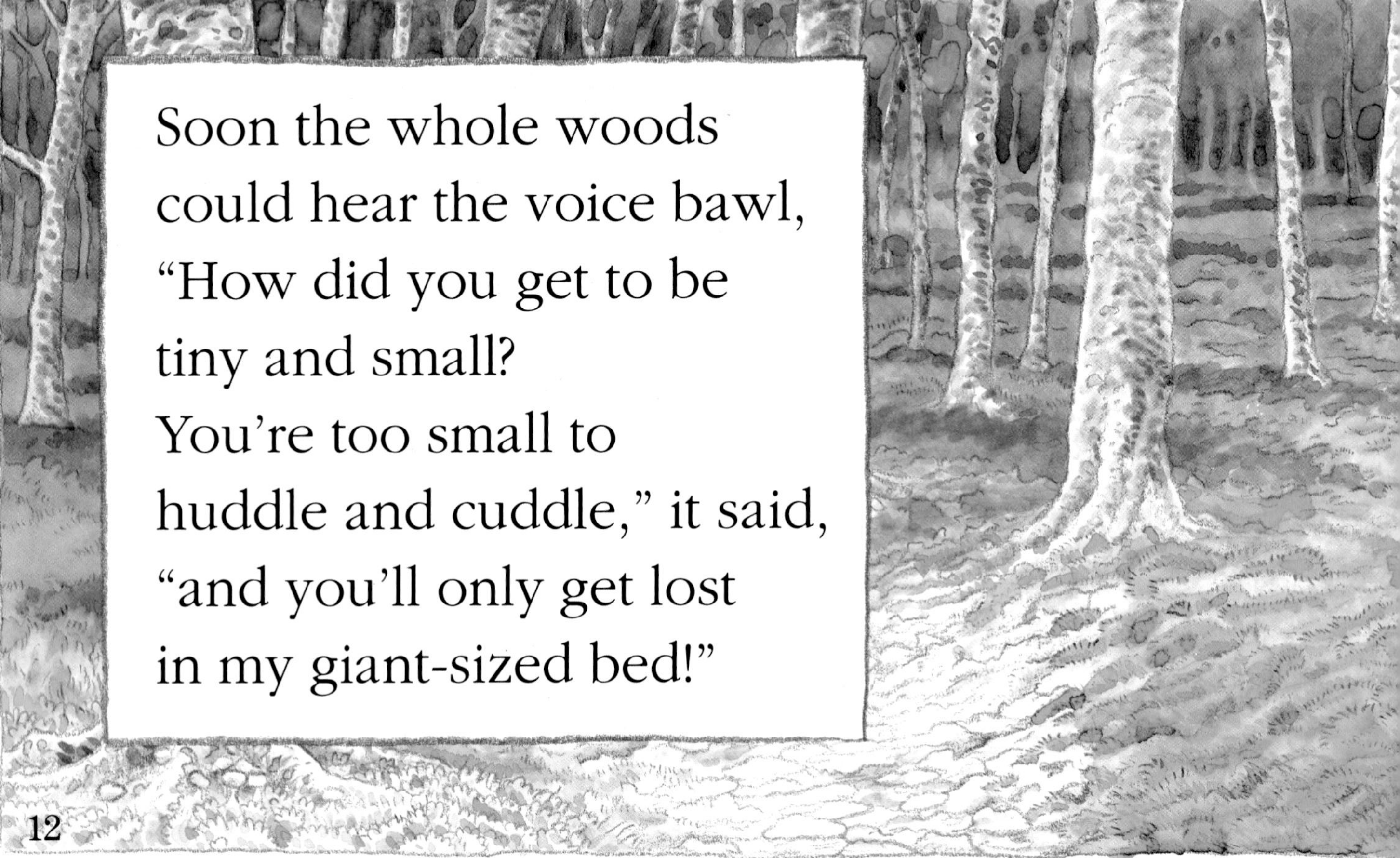

Soon the whole woods
could hear the voice bawl,
"How did you get to be
tiny and small?
You're too small to
huddle and cuddle," it said,
"and you'll only get lost
in my giant-sized bed!"

It was a gigantic bear
and a tiny teddy
stomping toward . . .

the giant teddy and Eddie.

"MY TED!"
gasped the bear.
"A BEAR!"
screamed Eddie.

“A BOY!”
yelled the bear.
“MY TEDDY!”
cried Eddie.

Then they ran and they ran
through the dark woods
back to their homes
as fast as they could . . .

all the way back
to their snuggly beds,
where they huddled
and cuddled their
own little teds.

JEZ ALBOROUGH has illustrated several books for children, including *Cuddly Dudley* and *Clothesline*. In 1985 he was runner-up for the prestigious Mother Goose Award. Jez Alborough says that while writing this book came easily, illustrating it did not because of all the scenery and the trees.